GALACTIC

Alan Durant

With illustrations by
Sue Mason

For my nephew and niece,
Christopher and Caroline

First published in 2015 in Great Britain by
Barrington Stoke Ltd
18 Walker Street, Edinburgh, EH3 7LP

www.barringtonstoke.co.uk

4u2read edition based on *Game Boy Galactic*
(Barrington Stoke, 2009)

Text © 2015 Alan Durant
Illustrations © 2009/2015 Sue Mason

A CIP catalogue record for this book is available
from the British Library upon request

ISBN: 978-1-78112-473-4

Printed in China by Leo

Contents

Level 1

Muzzy ran. He had to. Soldiers were on their way to his village. They would take any man or boy they found and shoot them. Muzzy's mum had told him to run. So now Muzzy and his dad were here in the dark, running for their lives.

Kaboom!

Something exploded on the road behind Muzzy. Muzzy's feet slipped and he fell. This was it. He couldn't run any more. He started to cry.

"Muzzy!" Muzzy's dad grabbed his arm and yanked him up. "Muzzy, run! You have to run!" His dad pushed him on.

Muzzy ran.

Muzzy and his dad ran and ran. First they ran into the hills. Then they ran to the border of their country. They ran from the enemy soldiers and they ran from the border police. They ran and ran ...

At last they found a lorry with its back doors open. They jumped in and hid in a small space behind some big wooden boxes. The doors shut and the lorry drove away.

Muzzy and his dad were in the lorry for a long time. It was very dark and it was hard to breathe. Muzzy wanted to scream but he had to be as silent as a butterfly – like the ones in the field by his village where he and his sisters played.

At last the lorry stopped. The doors opened. Light came in. Air.

Muzzy and his dad were in another country. They had escaped. Now they were refugees.

And, for Muzzy, that was just the start of his problems.

Level 2

Muzzy went to school in his new country but he found it hard. It wasn't easy to make friends. Some children laughed at him. They told him to go back to where he came from. That was what Muzzy wanted more than anything. But he couldn't go back. He had to stay here with his dad until the war in their own country was over and it was safe to return.

Muzzy was a fast learner. Soon he could speak and read in his new language. Some nights he even dreamed in it. He had many bad dreams about the soldiers. But the worst dreams were about the lorry.

There was a boy at school called J.P. He was kind to Muzzy. One day he gave Muzzy a present. It was a Game Boy.

"I don't use it any more," he said. "You can have it."

Muzzy was amazed when J.P. turned the Game Boy on and showed him how to play a game.

"Thanks," Muzzy said and he did something very rare – he smiled.

Muzzy and his dad lived in a room in a house with other refugees. Muzzy's dad had a job working as a bin man. It was a bit dirty and smelly, but Muzzy's dad didn't mind. He knew how hard it was to find work.

That evening, Muzzy showed his dad the Game Boy that J.P. had given him.

"I'm glad you're making friends," his dad said.

The next evening Muzzy's dad had a surprise for Muzzy.

"Look what I found at the tip," he said.

It was a Game Boy game! It didn't have a title on it, just one line of print. Muzzy read the words out loud.

"WARNING! THIS GAME MAY BE
VERY BAD FOR YOU."

What did that mean?

On the way to school next morning Muzzy put the new game in his Game Boy.

"Hi Muzzy!" A girl called out to him as he walked by. It was Mia, with her little brother Zak.

Muzzy thought of his own sisters as he waved to Mia and Zak. He missed playing with them.

All of a sudden Muzzy had a weird feeling that someone was watching him. He looked across the street. There was a man in a phone box staring at him. The man was wearing thick glasses. His eyes were huge and seemed to gleam. He had a cone of white hair on top of his head. He smiled at Muzzy, and the smile gave Muzzy the creeps. He walked faster.

Muzzy's Game Boy pinged as the game loaded up. A new message flashed up on the screen.

WARNING! ONCE YOU START THERE
IS NO GOING BACK.

'That's true,' Muzzy thought. He couldn't go back, could he?

"Muzz-ee! Muzz-ee!" Some voices called out behind Muzzy. Not friends this time. The nasty, mocking bullies from school.

Muzzy ran.

Level 3

The game was still on in Muzzy's hand as he ran. The screen showed a strange red land with red mist rising from the ground. Then Muzzy looked up again.

"Wh-what?" he stuttered.

Puffs of red mist were rising all around. The pavement was gone. The ground was red earth now, not concrete. The bullies were nowhere to be seen.

Muzzy looked down at his hands and saw the Game Boy game was no longer there. He stopped running and looked around. It was like he had been sucked into the game and was playing it from the inside! But how could that be? And where was he now?

Something glinted in the mist ahead. Muzzy moved towards it and came to a pile of rocks. The glinting thing was a shiny stone, a crystal. Muzzy bent down and picked it up. The crystal glowed in his hand. It made

Muzzy feel warm and strong. He remembered the game J.P. had given him. It had tokens to collect to help you win the game. Perhaps this crystal was like that.

Muzzy put the crystal in his pocket and spotted another one up ahead. Soon he had picked up six of them. But then he forgot all about the crystals – there was a space-ship in the sky!

The space-ship made a loud hum in the air. It had a kind of metal arm that moved

from side to side. Right now it was pointing at Muzzy. At the end of the arm was a huge green jelly eye. It was staring right at Muzzy. It made him shiver.

There was a whooshing noise and a beam of light shot out from the space-ship and hit the ground in front of Muzzy with a flash of fire. Muzzy jumped back. If that beam had hit him, he would have been burned up! Someone was trying to kill him!

Muzzy threw himself behind a tall pile of rocks.

Whoosh! The space-ship fired again.

Crash! The rocks were blown away.

Muzzy wasn't hurt but now he had nowhere to hide.

The huge green eye was looking for him again – what could he do? His eyes fixed on some pillars of red mist. Perhaps he could hide inside one of those? For a second he wondered if the mist might be a poison gas, but he didn't have any choice.

Muzzy sprinted to the nearest pillar of mist, waited for a second, then stepped inside. The red mist swirled round him.

Muzzy heard the hum of the space-ship and waited for a blast of fire ... but none came. The hum moved away. But Muzzy was pretty sure it would come back. He couldn't stay here for ever.

Muzzy peeked out at the red land around him. There was a large hill in the distance. If this was some sort of game, then perhaps that was where he had to go to complete the level.

Muzzy waited until he heard the hum of the space-ship move further away, then he dashed to the next pillar of mist. It closed round him like a cloak. The space-ship couldn't see him.

Muzzy made his way towards the hill, moving from misty pillar to misty pillar. It took a long time, because the space-ship kept coming back as it searched for him. J.P.'s game had a time limit and if you went over it, you lost tokens or a life. Muzzy hoped he wouldn't lose any of his shiny stones. Or die.

At last, Muzzy was inside the last pillar of mist and the hill was right in front of him. But what now? Should he climb the hill? The space-ship's huge green eye would spot him and then he'd be an easy target for its killer beam.

Then he saw it – the mouth of a cave, half hidden behind rocks at the bottom of the hill. Muzzy didn't have to climb the hill, he had to get inside it!

The cave was about 50 metres away, much further than the distance between the misty pillars. Muzzy would have to move at just the right moment and run very fast ...

The space-ship hummed in the sky as it came closer. Muzzy started to run the instant the hum faded. He ran like he was being chased by the soldiers at home or the bullies in his new school. He ran for his life.

But five metres from the mouth of the cave, disaster struck – Muzzy tripped on a stone and fell over. His ankle hurt. He couldn't move.

The space-ship hum came closer.

Muzzy looked up and saw the big green jelly eye glaring down at him. Then he heard his dad's voice in his head, "Muzzy, get up, run! You have to run!"

Muzzy tried to ignore the pain in his ankle as he pulled himself to his feet and ran. His heart thumped. Would he make it? He heard the whoosh of the beam and threw himself forward into the cave. Fire scorched his feet. Then everything went black.

Level 4

Muzzy blinked. He had expected it to be dark inside the hill, but it was light. There was a whole new world in there. Muzzy must have moved up a level in the game. How many more levels would there be?

In the beautiful garden in front of Muzzy, the plants and leaves were purple instead of green. They were strange shapes too. There were plants that looked like elephants' trunks, giant bells, cabbages on sticks and huge sharp spears.

Muzzy knew that this was a game and he would have to play in some way. He felt in his pocket. Three of the six stones had gone. He must have been right about the time penalty in the last level. He would have to move faster.

Muzzy made his way through the tall plants. He hadn't gone far when he saw that he was in a maze. So, that was the game!

Muzzy needed to put down a marker of some kind, so that he wouldn't keep going back along the same path.

In school he'd read a story about a Greek hero who had to go into a maze to kill a monster. When the monster was dead, the hero escaped by following the thread he had put down as he went into the maze.

What could Muzzy use? He looked around and saw vines growing on one of the plants. He pulled hard and a long line of vine came away. Muzzy coiled it around his arm. Then he dropped one end of the vine behind him and started off again.

Muzzy walked fast. He went up and down the paths of the maze. He seemed to be going in towards the middle. Maybe he'd been lucky and chosen the right way first time.

But then he came to a dead end. He broke off the vine then walked back the way he'd come until he found another path he hadn't been down before. He let the vine trail behind him again. He came to another dead end ... and another.

Muzzy stopped in front of a wall of bright flowers. They were like the water lilies that grew in his village pond. They were yellow in the middle with bright purple petals. His sisters called them gas jets, because that's what they looked like – jets of flame on a gas stove. Muzzy reached out a hand to touch one.

"Ah!" Muzzy cried out. The flowers were hot like flames and they had burned his hand! He blew on his hand and shook it.

This place wasn't like home. Muzzy couldn't trust anything here. He put his hand in his pocket and wasn't surprised to find that another of the crystal stones had gone.

Muzzy walked down another path, and another. He took care not to touch the sides of the maze where the bright flowers grew. He was getting tired. He must be near the middle of the maze – and what then? What would he find there? What if he were walking into a trap? But he had no choice. His only way out was to keep looking for the middle.

Muzzy had no more vine left to put down as a marker. He looked around for something else to use. There was another plant with leaves like rope on the maze wall in front of him. That would do. He reached up and grabbed at it.

All of a sudden, arms sprang out from the plant and grabbed Muzzy. They wrapped around him like the tentacles of an octopus and started to crush him. Muzzy felt faint. He struggled but the tentacles were too strong. They were squeezing the life out of him. He didn't even have enough air in his lungs to cry out. He was running out of time.

Muzzy was about to give up hope when an idea came into his head. With one last effort he turned in the grip of the octopus plant and

pushed back so that one of its arms rubbed against the gas-jet flowers. In seconds the arm burst into flame! There was a terrible screech and the arms let go of their grip on Muzzy. He rolled free. Then he got to his feet and ran.

The next path Muzzy went down took him to the middle of the maze. He ran on. The maze vanished.

Level 5

Muzzy took a deep breath. He'd got onto another level – but only just. What dangers would he face now?

In front of him the ground was bumpy, cracked and orange like honey-comb. On his right, bright yellow steamy springs shot up. To his left, pools of brown mud bubbled like hot chocolate. Beyond all of this, a huge, silver dome shone in the sun.

Muzzy was sure that he had to get to the dome. That must be the heart of this strange game.

Muzzy started to walk again, on a path between the springs and the mud. He felt a bit like a girl called Dorothy in a film they'd watched at school one wet lunch time. *The Wizard of Oz*, it was called.

Dorothy had to follow the yellow brick road – Muzzy had to follow the orange cracked path. It was a nice thought. The film had a happy ending. As Muzzy thought about it, he felt more relaxed ... too relaxed. He didn't see the things slithering out of the cracks in the ground, until it was almost too late.

They were disgusting. They were red, squashy and slimy like slugs but hairy too like caterpillars. They had long feelers at the front and they hissed as they slithered. Muzzy heard them before he saw them. He looked down and saw one of them slither over his left foot. He kicked hard, but it held on. He kicked at the giant bug with his right foot and it flicked off into the air with an angry squeal.

Muzzy felt a sharp prick at the back of his left leg, just above the ankle. He looked down

and saw another of the bugs on his leg. He
cried out and whacked it away with his hand.
It left a trickle of blood on his skin where it had
pricked him.

The bugs were all around Muzzy now. He
couldn't get to the silver dome this way. He'd
have to choose the yellow springs or the mud
pools. But which one? There was steam rising
from the springs and so Muzzy was sure they
must be burning hot. The mud pools then.

Muzzy ran towards the pools and was about
to step in when he stopped.

What if there were other things in the
bubbling mud? The pools were so dark he
couldn't see what might be hiding in them.
Back in his own country, one of Muzzy's friends
had been killed when he stepped on a land-
mine that he hadn't seen. No, Muzzy would
much rather see any danger that was waiting
for him.

Muzzy turned, jumped over a swarm of the giant bugs and ran across to the yellow springs. He stopped for a moment to watch. He saw how the springs came out of the ground, got taller and taller, made an arch, and then dropped down again. There was a second's break and then they shot up once more.

Muzzy could feel the heat of the springs from where he was standing. He was sure the yellow water would give him a bad burn if it went on his skin. But how could he get through the springs without getting burned?

He thought about the controls on a Game Boy. In a Game Boy game, what would he do? Of course, he'd roll!

As soon as the yellow springs started to rise and make their arches, he'd roll and hope that he'd be fast enough to get through before they dropped back down.

Muzzy needed to act fast because the giant bugs were slithering closer. And not only that – a monster was rising from out of the mud pool!

The monster roared. Muzzy threw himself forward and rolled for his life.

Drops from the yellow springs fell all around him, spitting and sizzling like acid. Steam scorched his ears, but he kept rolling, over and over. He was almost at the end of the springs. They were dropping now – fast. Muzzy closed his eyes and threw himself forward.

Muzzy landed with a bump on the dry ground. He'd made it! On the other side of the springs, the mud monster was beating its chest and roaring. Its teeth were huge. Thank goodness Muzzy hadn't chosen to go through the mud pools!

He got to his feet and ran towards the silver dome.

Another level done.

Level 6

Above the gates to the silver dome a red warning sign flashed, ENTER AT YOUR PERIL!

Muzzy didn't need to be told that there would be danger in the dome! The last stone had gone from his pocket. He must have lost it when the bug sucked his blood. So now he had nothing to help him. He was all on his own.

Muzzy walked over to the gates and they slid open. He stepped inside.

It was amazing. There were cameras and screens everywhere. Muzzy looked up at a screen and saw himself on it! He waved. The little Muzzy on the screen waved too. Muzzy and his dad had an old TV in their house. The picture was fuzzy, but every night they watched the news. They always hoped for good news from their home country.

A few steps ahead of Muzzy, big silver escalators flowed up and down. Muzzy loved escalators. The first time he saw one, in his new country, he ran up and down, up and down until he was dizzy.

At the top of the escalators was a square platform. That must be where Muzzy had to go.

Muzzy stepped onto the escalator to go up. He watched himself on the screens as he climbed. He grinned and pulled silly faces. He stuck out his tongue and ... what was that?

An alien appeared on the screen behind him. It had a warty green face with one glowing red eye. It was holding a gun ... and the gun was aimed at Muzzy!

Muzzy threw himself down. A burst of flame passed over his head. He looked up and on the screen he saw the alien moving away. It must have been on another escalator – going down. Muzzy had been too busy staring into the screens to see it. And now another alien with a gun was coming his way!

Muzzy got ready. When they were level with each other, the alien raised his gun and fired. But Muzzy had already ducked down and the gun-fire passed over his head with no harm done.

Muzzy shook himself into action. He started running up the escalator. Each time he drew level with an alien, he ducked down. He had to get his timing just right ... and he did it. He got to the top of the escalator and jumped onto the platform.

Muzzy looked about him. There were tunnels like tubes all around the dome. In the middle was a giant crystal. Muzzy was sure that's where he needed to go.

There was a kind of car in front of Muzzy. It was small and on the side it said Pod 327. More aliens were heading for Muzzy. Muzzy didn't waste a second. He climbed inside the pod car. The roof closed over him. The controls lit up. On the control panel a word flashed in red.

DRIVE.

Muzzy put his foot on the pedal. The car shot forward.

The pod car sped down a tunnel. Muzzy steered to the left and then to the right. He was going towards the giant crystal. When he got there he might find out how to get out of this game. How long had he been on this alien planet?

"Hey!" Muzzy yelled as something swooped down at him. It was a sort of metal bird with a beak like a spear-head. Muzzy swerved just in time.

Clank! The bird's metal beak hit the side of the pod. It left a dent in it.

Muzzy turned another corner. More of the metal birds flew at him.

Muzzy looked down at the controls. There was a red button on the wheel. He pushed it.

Tatata-tatata-tatata-tat!

A line of bullets fired from the front of the car. As the birds came nearer, he pushed the button again.

Tatata-tatata-tatata-tat!

The birds exploded.

Muzzy steered the car into another tunnel. More birds swooped at him. He waited till they were close and then pushed the red button.

Tatata-tatata-tatata-tat! Tatata-tatata-tatata-tat!

Bird after bird exploded.

But more birds appeared. In a few moments there were too many for Muzzy to shoot them all.

He turned into other tunnels, left and right, left and right, on a round-about route to the giant crystal. It seemed to work. After a while, the birds stopped swooping. Muzzy was glad. The birds and their spear-beaks had been scary.

But Muzzy still wasn't safe.

All of a sudden another pod car sped along the tunnel towards him.

Muzzy pushed the button and fired his guns, but a shield went up at the front of the other pod and the bullets bounced off. The pod sped closer and fired its gun at Muzzy. He had no time to get out of the way of the bullets. He looked down at the controls. There was a green button. He pushed it. A shield popped up. The bullets from the other pod hit the shield with a *pop-pop-pop*. But they didn't break it. Muzzy wasn't hurt.

But Muzzy wasn't out of danger yet. The other pod was still speeding on and it was aiming right at him. It wasn't going to stop. It was going to crash right into Muzzy's pod!

Muzzy held the wheel steady. He had to be strong and brave. He must not flinch or turn too early. He had to keep his nerve.

The two pods raced towards each other. On and on they rushed. Muzzy was sure that they would crash ...

Right at the very last moment, Muzzy turned the wheel hard to the left and his pod swerved away. The other pod carried on down the tunnel and round the corner. Muzzy took a deep breath. That had been too close – much too close.

He drove on to the end of the tunnel and turned right. There it was – the giant crystal!

Level 7

Inside the crystal, light gleamed, glinted, sparkled and flashed everywhere. Muzzy was amazed.

A huge blank screen hung from the roof. There were no aliens, no metal birds or slithering bugs or swamp monsters. That was good.

Muzzy was tired. He didn't have the energy to fight any more. He just wanted the game to end, so that he could go home. But then he thought about the bullies waiting for him.

Why was everyone always chasing him? What had he ever done wrong? He hadn't hurt anyone. All he wanted was to live in peace – to go home. But where was home?

As if in answer to Muzzy's question, a message flashed up on the screen.

You have played well. Pass the final test and you may leave this galaxy and go home. The Controller.

Muzzy blinked. "How?" he said aloud.

A new message appeared.

You must face your fear.

Muzzy shook his head. Face his fear! How many more fears did he have to face?

Another message.

Your true fear. Face it and you will be free. Run from it and you will die.

44

The words melted away and pictures formed on the screen of alien guards with guns, marching up to the giant crystal.

Muzzy couldn't run any longer. He was trapped. He'd have to face his fear. But after all Muzzy had been through, how bad could that be? He could face anything.

"Tell me what I must do," he said to the screen.

The answer came at once.

Enter the box and lift the galactic diamond.

Muzzy frowned. What box?

Then he saw it – a small opening that led into a narrow tunnel. At the end was a box just big enough for Muzzy to fit into. A tiny, dark space with no air, like the lorry where he and his dad had hidden.

Muzzy stared at the box in horror. Already he was gasping for air, his heart was racing, and his hands and face were wet with sweat.

He couldn't do it.

A loud noise made Muzzy look back at the screen. The guards were almost at the door to the giant crystal. In a few moments they would

be inside and Muzzy would have no chance.
There were hundreds of them, all with one
aim – to kill him.

Muzzy started to shake. This was the
nightmare he feared more than any other. If
we went into that box, there was no way he
could get out.

The doors to the crystal began to slide open.

Another wave of panic hit Muzzy.

He couldn't do it.

But he had to.

"Go on, Muzzy!" In his head, his dad's voice
pushed him on.

The doors were almost open.

Muzzy looked up at the screen. 'It's a game,
Muzzy,' he told himself. 'Don't let a game beat
you!'

As the first alien entered the giant crystal, Muzzy squeezed into the tunnel. It was so narrow that he could hardly move. But he forced himself on ... One last wriggle and he was inside the box.

The galactic diamond glowed in the dark, stuffy space. Muzzy tried to breathe, but there was no air. He reached out a shaky hand and grabbed the diamond.

For a moment it seemed that nothing was going to happen. Then the dark exploded into light – and Muzzy's lungs filled with air. His feet touched concrete.

He'd done it. He'd escaped!

Level 8

Muzzy looked at the screen.

WELL DONE! YOU HAVE WON!
WANT TO PLAY AGAIN?

Muzzy didn't feel like he'd won. He'd only just escaped. No way did he want to play again!

"Muzz-ee! Muzz-ee!"

Muzzy was back with the bullies. They were right behind him now. He started running. But then he stopped.

Muzzy had escaped from soldiers back home and from the scariest game in the world. What were a few bullies compared to that?

It was time to stop running. It was time to face his fear.

Muzzy turned and the bullies almost ran into him.

"What you got there, Muzzy?" the leader of the bullies said. He pointed at the Game Boy in Muzzy's hand.

"J.P. gave it to me," Muzzy said. "He's my friend."

"You ain't got no friends," the bully sneered. "You should go back home. We don't want you here."

Muzzy looked the bully in the eye. "This is my home now," he said. "I'm not an alien. I live here like you."

The bullies looked at each other. They didn't seem to know what to do. The leader took a step forward.

"What game are you playing?" he demanded.

"My dad found it," Muzzy said. "But it's more than just a game. It's scary."

The bullies laughed.

"You'd better give it to me then," the leader said. "We don't want little Muzzy scared by a bit of rubbish."

"You don't want it," Muzzy said. "It's bad. It could kill you."

The bullies thought this was the funniest thing ever.

"I mean it," Muzzy insisted.

The bully held out his hand. "Give it to me," he said.

"OK, if you really want it," Muzzy said. He took the game out and handed it to the bully.

"Cheers, Muzz-ee," the bullies crowed and they marched away.

"Hey, Muzzy!" It was J.P. He walked up to Muzzy, grinning. Muzzy grinned back. He felt a wave of happiness. He belonged.

Across the street, the man with the cone of white hair watched the two boys walk away together. He smiled and, behind his thick glasses, his odd eyes glinted like diamonds.